For Maya and Elliot
with love!
—A.S.C.

I Can Read® and I Can Read Book® are trademarks of HarperCollins Publishers.

Biscuit Visits the Firehouse
Text copyright © 2024 by Alyssa Satin Capucilli.
Illustrations copyright © 2024 by Pat Schories.
All rights reserved. Manufactured in Malaysia.
No part of this book may be used or reproduced in any manner whatsoever without written permission except
in the case of brief quotations embodied in critical articles and reviews. For information address HarperCollins
Children's Books, a division of HarperCollins Publishers, 195 Broadway, New York, NY 10007.
www.icanread.com

Library of Congress Control Number: 2023944812
ISBN 978-0-06-326665-0 (trade bdg.) — ISBN 978-0-06-326664-3 (pbk.)

Book design by Marisa Rother

24 25 26 27 28 COS 10 9 8 7 6 5 4 3 2 1 First Edition

Biscuit Visits the Firehouse

story by ALYSSA SATIN CAPUCILLI
pictures by ROSE MARY BERLIN
in the style of PAT SCHORIES

HARPER
An Imprint of HarperCollinsPublishers

Here we are, Biscuit.

We're going to the firehouse.

Woof, woof!

This way, Biscuit.

Our friends are coming too.

Woof!

Bow wow!

Bow wow!

Wait for us, Biscuit.

The firehouse is very big.

Clang, clang! Clang, clang!

The bell is big and shiny!

Woof, woof!

11

Funny puppy!

You found the firefighters'

shiny helmets.

Woof!

You found their

tall boots, too.

Over here, Biscuit.

There's a lot to see

at the firehouse.

I hope we can meet

the firefighters soon.

Woof!

Here they come now!

Woof, woof!

This way, Biscuit.

It's time to see

the fire truck.

Let's climb aboard

Woof!

The fire truck has a long hose
to spray water, Biscuit.

There's a tall ladder,

for climbing, too.

21

Woo-woo! Woo-woo!

Biscuit! Come back.

Woof, woof, woof, woof!

That's the fire truck's loud siren.

Woof!

What do you see now,

Biscuit?

Woof, woof!

You found a bone.

But whose can it be?

Ruff!

Sweet puppy!

You found Dottie.

Dottie helps
at the firehouse, too.
Woof!
Ruff!

We learned a lot

about the firehouse, Biscuit.

And we made new friends, too.

Bow wow!

Woof, woof!

Ruff!

Clang, clang! Clang, clang!